Where's That Reptile?

by Barbara Brenner and Bernice Chardiet
Illustrated by Carol Schwartz

Cartwheel
·B·O·O·K·S· ™

SCHOLASTIC INC.

New York Toronto London Auckland Sydney

Introduction

Some of them creep,
Some of them crawl,
Some of them have
No legs at all.

Some have shells,
They all have scales.
Some have rattles
On their tails.

A few can leave
Their tails behind!
Look, look, look!
And you will find.

The Great Turtle Race

These teeny, tiny leatherback turtles just hatched from their eggs. Now they must race to the ocean before hungry gulls or crabs can grab them. Have any of the turtles reached the water? Can you see five?

It's a Fact:
Leatherbacks are the largest sea turtles in the world. They can grow to be as big as rowboats and weigh up to 1900 pounds. The females come ashore only to lay their eggs. Then they go back to the sea. The baby leatherbacks run to the water as soon as they hatch.

What Color Is This Lizard?

Sometimes they're green. Sometimes they're brown. Anole (say "a-NO-lee") lizards can change color! How many green anoles do you see in the big picture? And can you find two male anoles? They're the ones with the fanned-out throat sacs.

It's a Fact:
There are more than 300 different kinds of anoles. This one is called the American chameleon. It can change color as if by magic. The males fan out their throat sacs to attract a female or to scare another male.

Big Mouths!

Here is a whole gang of Nile crocodiles. As you can see, they sleep with their mouths open. Look at those teeth! They are sharp enough to tear into a hippopotamus's hide.

It's a Fact:
Mother crocodiles are very gentle with their own babies. The mother crocodile carries her babies in her mouth. Can you find a baby in this picture?

It's a Monitor Attack!

A monitor lizard is sneaking up on
the crocodile nest. Monitor lizards eat
crocodile eggs. The monitor lizard
looks a little like a small dinosaur.
But two sleeping crocs are nearby. Do
you see them?

It's a Fact:
How do you know when a monitor
lizard is mad? It opens its mouth,
blows out its neck, and hisses. Then
it lashes its tail like a whip. By that
time, you'd better leave! A monitor
lizard can run faster than a person.

Snug as a Snake

Watch out! Rattlesnakes! They're poisonous! Is there one big snake in the den or are there lots of snakes? How many heads can you find? How many rattler tails can you count?

It's a Fact:
A rattlesnake keeps growing rattles as long as it lives. Some rattlesnakes have as many as 30 rattles! When a rattlesnake shakes its tail, it makes a noise. That's a warning!
It says, "Poisonous snake nearby!"

Alligator Swimming Hole

Alligators can grow to be 12 feet long
— longer than some picnic tables!
This alligator lives in a pond with
other alligators. It's going to the
water now. But can you find another
alligator that's already in the water?
Only its snout is sticking out so it
can breathe.

It's a Fact:
Crocodiles and alligators look very
much alike. It's hard to tell them
apart. The crocodile's upper and lower
teeth show when its mouth is closed.
The alligator's lower teeth do not.
Their snouts are different, too. And
crocodiles can move faster than
alligators.

Is There a Gecko in the House?

Most geckos live outside. But tree geckos, like this one, often live in houses. People don't mind having it around because it clears the house of insects. In fact, there it is, eating a moth right now. Do you see it?

It's a Fact:
Geckos are great climbers. They have hooks on the undersides of their toes that are so tiny they are almost invisible. They can even climb up a piece of glass. Geckos are lizards.

The Disappearing Act

Here's another kind of gecko. It's called a leaf-tailed gecko and it can do a disappearing act. It's resting somewhere on one of these branches, but it looks like a leaf. Can you find it?

It's a Fact:
Geckos live in warm places all around the world. This kind of gecko lives on the island of Madagascar, off the coast of Africa.

The Snake Vine

This snake looks just like a vine on the tree. Which is the vine? Which is the vine snake? Do you see a little lizard, too? That lizard had better watch out!

It's a Fact:
Vine snakes eat mainly lizards and birds. But snakes don't chew. The vine snake has fangs in its mouth that poison its prey. Then the snake swallows its dinner whole!

Horned Toad Hideout

The horned toad isn't really a toad. It's a lizard. Sometimes it lies half buried in the sand. Can you find a horned toad hiding here? The roadrunner can.

It's a Fact:
Horned toads have different patterns
and colors. They're hard to see
because they blend in with their
surroundings. Their spiky armor
protects them from enemies like
snakes and birds.

Snake Birthday Party

These baby garter snakes have just been born. Can you see the mama snake? There are more than 20 babies — many more. How many heads do you count?

It's a Fact:
Most snakes lay eggs. But the garter snake gives birth to live babies. There can be as many as 85 babies in one litter. Newborn garter snakes are about 6 to 10 inches long. Garter snakes are not harmful to humans.

An Iguana Tale

Here's a tree full of iguanas. One of them almost got eaten when a bird caught him. It had to leave its tail behind to get away! Can you find the iguana with the missing tail?

It's a Fact:
Iguanas and many other lizards can part with their tails to save their lives. No problem! A new tail will grow back!

The Snapping Turtle Trick

The alligator snapping turtle has a trick. Its tongue can wiggle like a worm. When a foolish fish swims over to take a look — *snap*! Can you find that sneaky snapper? How many other creatures do you see?

It's a Fact:
A full-grown snapping turtle can weigh over 200 pounds. It has powerful jaws and claws for catching and holding food. It's slow in the water and it stays away from people who are swimming. But on land — don't mess with a snapping turtle! It can hurt you.

Turtle Roundup

There are about 200 different species (kinds) of turtles. Some live in water. Turtles that live only on land are called tortoises. Here are just a few of them.

Find the turtle that looks as if someone painted it. You can see why it's called a painted turtle.

Now find one with a very high shell. It's called a box turtle.

Can you find a spotted turtle? It looks just like its name!

Look for the red-eared slider. But don't look for ears. Turtles don't have any!

The one eating a cactus is the desert tortoise. Can you find it?

It's a Fact:
Turtles were around at the time of the dinosaurs. Tortoises — land turtles — live a very long time. Some are more than 100 years old. One tortoise actually lived 152 years.

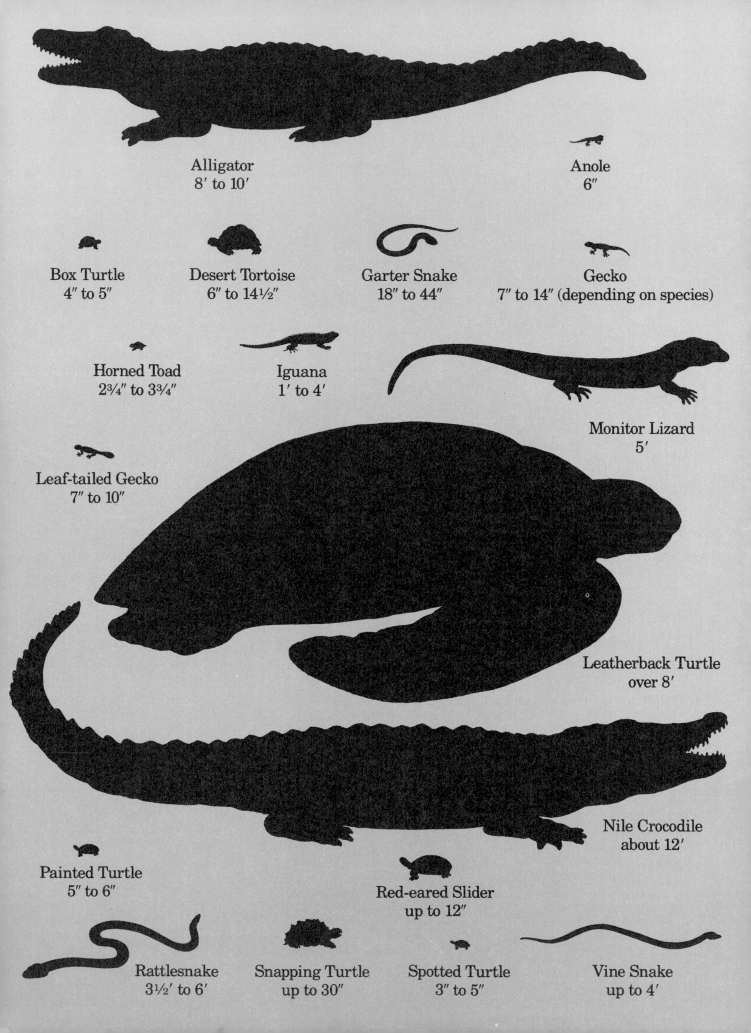

Alligator
8′ to 10′

Anole
6″

Box Turtle
4″ to 5″

Desert Tortoise
6″ to 14½″

Garter Snake
18″ to 44″

Gecko
7″ to 14″ (depending on species)

Horned Toad
2¾″ to 3¾″

Iguana
1′ to 4′

Monitor Lizard
5′

Leaf-tailed Gecko
7″ to 10″

Leatherback Turtle
over 8′

Nile Crocodile
about 12′

Painted Turtle
5″ to 6″

Red-eared Slider
up to 12″

Rattlesnake
3½′ to 6′

Snapping Turtle
up to 30″

Spotted Turtle
3″ to 5″

Vine Snake
up to 4′